# INTIMACY

West Palm Beach, Florida

## LEOSTONE MORRISON

Copyright © 2021 Leostone Morrison

All rights reserved. No part of this publication may be reproduced, copied, stored in a retrieval system, transmitted, scanned in any form or under any conditions, including, photocopying, electronic, recording, or otherwise, without the written permission of the author, Leostone Morrison. For permission requests, contact Leostone Morrison at restorativeauthor@gmail.com

ISBN: 978-1-954755-10-9

Published by:
Restoration of the Breach without Borders
133 45th Street, Building A7
West Palm Beach, Florida 33407
restorativeauthor@gmail.com
Tele: (561) 388-2949

EBook Cover Design by: Calbert Simson
divine.creativevillage@gmail.com

Editing done by: Melisha Bartley-Ankle
melbarxtd@yahoo.com

Picture drawing done by: Moneque Graham-Edwards
monequegraham1@gmail.com

Formatting and Publishing done by: Sherene Morrison
Publisher.20@aol.com

Unless otherwise stated Scripture verses are quoted from the King James Version of the Bible.

# TABLE OF CONTENTS

| | |
|---|---:|
| **Chapter 1: Intimacy** | 1 |
| **Chapter 2: Elements That Ignite Intimacy** | 12 |
| **Chapter 3: The Little Things** | 26 |
| **Chapter 4: Intimate Language** | 37 |
| **Chapter 5: Errors Of Comparison** | 42 |
| **Chapter 6: Complaints** | 49 |
| **Chapter 7: "Is It Really A Sin?"** | 60 |
| **Chapter 8: Sex Toys** | 71 |
| **Chapter 9: Divine Pleasure** | 76 |
| **Chapter 10: Work Of Art** | 90 |
| **Chapter 11: Sexual Positions** | 97 |
| **Chapter 12: Game Time** | 98 |
| Conclusion | 116 |
| About The Author | 120 |

# DEDICATION

This book is dedicated to marriages ordained by God.

# ACKNOWLEDGEMENT

To the Holy Spirit my Primary Destiny Helper. I am ecstatic to know that my assignment was not completed with the book- *Marriage Reconstruction* but continued *Marital Intimacy*. I am blessed with the family I have. Sherene, my wife; your support has no end and has only increased as the assignments from the Lord increases. You continue to prove that you are truly my gift from God.

Hillary Dunkley Campbell, you have come into my life for such a time as this. Your kind words of endorsements are appreciated and your continued support with the assignments of Restoration of the Breach without Borders Ministry. I thank you unsparingly.

To Aphia Brown, you are truly a divine destiny helper. You are appreciated. Thank you for your endorsement and encouragement to this book.

To Donna Satahoo, you have proven yourself to be a staple in my life. You are loved and appreciated. Thank you for your endorsement for this book on marriages.

My mentor Rev. David Grant, your support has not ceased since I met you as a newly converted Christian. I thank you for writing such a beautiful foreword. I pray you will continue to make yourself available to the Kingdom of God. I look forward to continued partnership.

# ENDORSEMENTS

Intimacy in marriage is a must read, the in-depth truth on what God allows within marriages and how a significant other meets the needs of their spouse, is deeply highlighted and broken down to its simplest form by Rev. Leostone Morrison with Gods biblical principles. This book will open up your knowledge and put your mind at ease about the do's and don'ts within your marriage and bedroom.

> Aphia Brown
> CEO
> Overcoming Through
> Christ Inc.

\* \* \* \*

This is a well needed book. Rev. Morrison with the help of the Holy Spirit has tapped into an area that is in dire need of help – *Marital Intimacy*. Intimacy is more than just sex. Many marriages, particularly Christian marriages, are experiencing an intimacy deficiency which have resulted in unhappy and unsatisfied spouses looking for intimacy in the wrong places and have led to many divorces. This book can be used as a guide to teach spouses how to truly experience real intimacy and not to be afraid to enjoy the gift that God has given them – each other.

>-Hillary Dunkley-Campbell
>Author
>*I Am Encouraged* 30 Days Devotional

# FOREWORD

Sexual fulfilment is a God-given right to each partner in the marital union. God created sensual points on the human body for the fulfilment of our sexual pleasure. The discovery of these points is an adventure always worth taking. You can and will be handsomely rewarded upon finding the "right" spot/spots.

Many Christians was introduced to sexual intimacy while in the world. Sex outside of marriage is fornication and carries guilt to an alive conscience. However, when we become Christians and are married many still hold that feeling of guilt and some even subconsciously believe the sex act is dirty and wrong.

In this book Leostone has brought to light the liberty and pleasure of sexual intimacy. As Christians we can glorify God through sexuality. The practical nature of this book may cause the reserved Christian to blush but I guarantee you upon completion of your reading this compelling work you will:

1. Be delivered from a restrictive mind-set.
2. See your sexual union in a transformative.
3. Give yourself freely to your partner.
4. Enjoy your partner.
5. Shout hallelujah during and after your time of sexual intimacy.

May read with an open mind and glorify God in your spirit and body which are HIS.

-David Grant
Founder of Odigia Global
Lead Pastor of Jamaica Evangelistic Centre

# INTRODUCTION

*Intimacy in marriage*

There are persons who are discouraged because they are single. They are tired of being the maid of honor or best man at weddings. And there are persons who are praying to get out of their marriage. Marriage comes embedded with much joy and challenges. The joys are quickly embraced and celebrated but the struggles are hated and prayed or wished away. Some of the more pronounced marital hatreds are found in the areas of finance, family, religion and intimacy. The focus of this discourse is intimacy within the confines of marriage. The first act of intimacy as recorded in the bible is found in Genesis 2:18, *"And God said, it is not good for man to be alone, I will create an help meet for him."* God saw that Adam had a need- intimacy. He was created perfect but lacked the comfort of intimate relationship. God gave him a wife from who his intimate needs would be supplied. This is not information to be treated casually. God supplied Adam's intimate needs within the confines of his marriage.

In Genesis 4:1-2 we read, *"Adam made love to his wife Eve, and she became pregnant and gave birth to Cain. She said, "With the help of the LORD I have brought forth a man."* Later she gave birth to his brother Abel. I find this very interesting as there is no record of sexual intimacy between Adam and his wife before they sinned. I do not believe that sexual intimacy was only available to them after they were put out of the Garden of Eden because in chapter 2:28 of Genesis, God commissioned them to be fruitful and replenish the earth. They were given the mandate to populate the earth with sons and daughters, which is a direct commandment from God to have sexual intimacy. Was Adam and Eve in disobedience to God and refrained from sexual intimacy or did God knowing that they would sin against Him, prevented pregnancy? Were they intimate but not sexually intimate? What is intimacy? I grew up believing that intimacy is within the parameters of kissing, caressing, or sucking of the breast, fondling of the bottom and penal penetration. As life continued, I became exposed to greater knowledge and truth as it relates to intimacy. I purpose to share on intimacy as wide and specific as I may. Please journey with me as we delve into greatness.

# CHAPTER 1
# INTIMACY

What is intimacy?

According to newmiddleclassdad.com INTIMACY is defined as an intimate act, especially sexual intercourse.

The definition says intimate act, especially sexual intercourse, meaning that it is not confined to sexual intercourse. Therefore, let us explore what the intimate act really is. Does intimacy require sexual intercourse? Can two persons in a consensual relationship be intimate without penial penetration? According to Mike Tucker in a 2015 article in All Posts Happy Marriage, "there are five forms of intimacy that every married couple needs in order to have a long and happy marriage. They are intellectual, social, emotional,

---

https://newmiddleclassdad.com/can-a-marriage-last-without-intimacy

spiritual and physical intimacy."

***Intellectual / cognitive intimacy*** *comes from exchanging thoughts and ideas openly. It has nothing to do with discussing highly intellectual ideas. There is a lot of intellectual stimulation to be gained from sharing your opinions about food, health, work and all the other things that affect our lives.*

A friend of mine told me she finds it sexy when she is intellectually stimulated. She tends to believe that when she is stimulated in this area, intimacy comes natural and easy for her because both persons are on the same wavelength.

*Social intimacy is about doing things together and generally experiencing life together. This includes things like taking a walk, making dinner or watching a movie with your spouse.*

Social intimacy will spruce up a relationship real fast. Especially if courting. Just making dinner or watching a movie, during that closeness, intimacy naturally has a way to happen. A kiss here and there during movie watching, holding of the hands etc. may lead to something more before dinner is through preparing.

*Emotional Intimacy is all about sharing feelings and emotions with each other. This form of intimacy can also be nurtured through empathizing with each other and trying to understand each other's feelings.*

Emotional intimacy is connection. It is a connection on a higher level, I believe. When two persons are emotionally intimate, the physicality of the moment is not even necessary especially if both are in a long distant relationship. That is where phone sex plays an important role. This is intimacy without penetration.

## MARITAL INTIMACY

*Spiritual intimacy comes from sharing religious beliefs and observing religious practices together. Christian couples can nurture spiritual intimacy by praying together, going to church together and reading and discussing the bible with one another.*

Spiritual intimacy can take on a new meaning if the married couple is having intimacy problems and are serious in wanting resolutions. Dominance and ignorance are two sexual sins in my book that will completely destroy intimacy. If this couple is on the same spiritual page and desire intimacy with each other, the first person to have consul with is God. The second person is your spouse. You will be guided by the Spirit of God and led by your love for your spouse to resolve any issues that may arise.

*Physical Intimacy can simply be described as "a loving touch." A loving touch, such as a hug or kiss communicates acceptance and love to your spouse. This in turn boosts the emotional connection between the two of you.*

Physical intimacy does not necessarily means sex. The second word is intimacy. Oftentimes intimacy is confused with sex. Two to five minutes of sex is surely not intimacy. Real satisfying and fulfilling intimacy is a combination of all factors above mentioned.

Intimacy therefore includes but is not limited to kissing, touching, erotic massage, and using sex toys. All these factors individually or collectively play important roles in arousing your partner, be it your husband or your wife. If intimacy is done correctly and interestingly, it does not have to stop at arousal but multiple orgasms.

## FOREPLAY

This love language is the foreplay of a potential intimate act. Foreplay does not necessarily mean an act before penial penetration. Foreplay starts out of the bedroom. It starts when you are in the office or in the grocery store. It starts when a picture of your partner in a seductive mood is sent to you.

Foreplay starts with words or actions that cultivate closeness within a union. Foreplay is not one size fits all. It is your song, your memory, or your style. It also starts with your eyes lock together from across the room sending an intimate message. Do you know that foreplay can determine the quality of intimacy in the bedroom?

I had a conversation some time ago with a female friend in the presence of my wife and she asked this question and proceed to an explanation. Can I be real with you? She says, have you ever had a thought of someone you had a sexual relationship with and you felt something move inside of you? Your vagina takes a somersault, or your penis twitches and your heart goes into tachycardia. If you continue to think of those sexual adventures, you become wet in your panties or hard in your underpants.

I am reminded of a passionate love story of a king and an unknown woman. King Solomon and the Shulamite woman his wife, who was the attention of his passion. A dear friend of mine said the words of Solomon just tickles her in places yet to be explored.

*"How beautiful are thy feet with shoes, O prince's daughter! The joints of thy thighs are like jewels, the work of the hands of a cunning workman. Thy navel is like a round goblet, which wanteth not liquor: thy belly is like a heap of wheat set about with lilies. Thy two breasts are like two young roes that are twins. Thy neck is as a tower of ivory; thine eyes like the fish pools in Heshbon, by the gate of Bathrabbim: thy nose is as the tower of Lebanon which looketh toward Damascus" (Songs of Solomon 7:1-6).*

MARITAL INTIMACY

# SEDUCTION (FROM MY POINT OF VIEW)

Seduction is an *intimate non-verbal language*. Wives, seduce your man with your eyes. Strip him slowly, very slowly, from his head to his toes. Let him know you want him. That you are wet for him. Let him know with your eyes he is the only man for you and if he is at an event with men, he is the only man there. Let your eyes make love to him.

Sit in a desirable position. Pretend you are just meeting your man for the first time. Let your eyes tell him. Also, use your body to seduce him. Slowly cross your leg by lifting a tot higher when doing so. You are telling him what you have is his. Husbands, this might sound crazy but listening to your wife is a powerful tool of seduction. A wife loves when her man is clean, well-groomed and smelling good. A fresh smelling breath is a major hit. It increases the possibility of intimacy several stairs up.

## NERVE POINTS

There are other options to intercourse and women are convinced that intimacy at times tops intercourse. Why? Because penile penetration does not always allow for orgasm for various reasons. These reasons can be painful sex, heavy menstruation, menopause, difficulty maintaining an erection. Additionally, penile penetration may not be the only prescription for clitoral stimulation. The clitoris is the pleasure center of the vulva. It can be stimulated from the outside and give as much pleasure and more than penile penetration.

There are nerve points that must be included in intimacy. If you want to bring your partner to a realm of satisfaction and fulfilment, use up these pressure areas in your love connections.

There are zones that are called extragenital erogenous zones. Now, these zones are the sensitive spots. They are loaded with nerve endings. For women, they are breasts, lips, clitoris, inner-thighs, neck and ears. These are the excitatory areas. You can either use your hands and/or mouth for stimulation. Your choice. Your goal is to satisfy, to have the orgasms coming. That is the ultimate in lovemaking.

For men, the extragenital erogenous zones are around the neck, the hairline, or the collarbone, nipples, balls, feet, and penis. Women, the teasing nibbling of the earlobes is a game changer. Additionally, caress the nape of his neck and nibble on those nipples. Intimacy should never be allowed to be imprisoned to sexual intercourse. I implore you as you continue on your journey of marital intimacy, that you explore intentionally the pleasure of intimacy.

Please note, intimacy is not for the emotionally unavailable (disconnected), nor is it for those who are in conflict with themselves. It is not child's play.

## CHAPTER 2
## ELEMENTS THAT IGNITE INTIMACY

Intimacy is a very integral part of our married life. Some key elements enhance our sexual intimacy. Ignorance and or lack of application of these elements can cause many frustrations and, in some cases, divorce. Rev. David Grant said he was invited to speak at a couples retreat a few years ago and while they were still in the devotional segment, an extremely frustrated wife began telling her story. Everyone there was taken aback as she took them all by surprise. Her face was painted with the look of absolute frustration. She got a blanket, placed it on the floor, laid on it, and began shouting at her husband to come on the blanket with her, showing how unromantic he was and devoid of intimacy. Of course, the organizers stepped in and gained control of the fiasco. The husband was publicly humiliated which certainly did further damage to his already bruised ego. When there is repeated intimate or sexual disappointment, the one being bottled can and will pop at some point. Pray it does not happen in the public sphere like the story just mentioned. There is a great need for education in this arena. We want to take a glance at a few of these elements here in this chapter.

## LOVE LANGUAGE

The subject of Love Languages was brought to light a few years ago by the distinguished Dr. Gary Chapman. He teaches that there are 5 Love Languages namely: Physical Touch, Time Spent, Gifts, Words of Affirmation, and Acts of Service. Knowing one's spouse's Love Language and "speaking" their language will greatly improve the intimacy in the marriage. A challenge that one can face in the area of love language, is speaking the wrong one. In the above story, the husband was a work-from-home husband. While being home, he would do most of the domestic chores. He would wash, cook, clean, and even bake. Oh, how my wife would love for me to bake. Many women would probably consider him the ideal catch. However, in her eyes, he was woefully lacking. They had been married at that time seventeen years and five of those years she had another man. Why? The other man was speaking her love language loud and clear. Her Love Language could be arranged in this order: Time Spent, Physical Touch, Words of Affirmation, Gifts, and then Acts of Service. Her husband seemed to have had them in this order: Acts of Service, Gifts, Time Spent, Physical Touch, and then Words of Affirmation. When you learn and give your spouse the language of love that they speak, it becomes so much easier for them to be intimate as their emotional walls are broken down through the power of genuine love.

As a couple it is important to understand your partner's love language' likes and dislikes. Achieving this positions you at an advantage for a happy marriage. There are woman whose love language is physical touch' while another might be affirmation of words' hence during love making she requires for her partner to speak to her in ways that will cause her love juices to flows. If she is not getting this then she might become unsatisfied with the love making process because both partners are speaking the same language.

With physical touch as a love language this partner might requires foreplay to get them in the moods for love making. After love making this partner will need to be held close to their spouse for a sense of fulfilment. We all experiences love and intimacy on different levels.

A partner whose love language is physical touch might require for you to hold her/him close or some form of cuddling after climax or orgasm as this will not only give satisfaction it makes him/her feels loved. Cuddling skin to skin after sexual intercourse allow couples to bond with each other. According to a 2016 survey from the Sex Information and Education Council of Canada and Trojan condoms, found that cuddling after sex can boost sexual satisfaction and increase closeness among couples. It is believed to be so because the body releases a hormone call oxytocin. Oxytocin is known as the love or cuddle hormone as it is said to be secreted by the posterior lobe of the pituitary gland a tiny structure at the base of the brain. This hormone is said to have gotten its name the love or cuddle hormone because it is released when people snuggle up or bond with each other. Intimacy goes back to having an open line for communication with your partner. Do not feel ashamed to say honey you are not pleasing me I would rather to be on top in the saddle position sometimes or let us try new positions because the missionary position is not working for me. The goal is not just for one person to climax but for both persons to feel satisfied and still feel the same way about each other or even more pleased with each other at the end of love making.

Remember most importantly you are team players and not each other's enemy. One wife said, speaking from the standpoint of a wife who values intimacy especially physical touch and words of affirmation; It is Important for you to maintain Intimacy after love making as this gives her the feeling of being special and also satisfied. Just that skin to skin contact after love making releases endorphins which causes her to sleep like a baby, waking up the next day wanting to take care of him and treat him like the king he is. The next time you make love with your partner you remember their love language. If it is acts of service, try to do something special for them, whether laundry' taking out the trash without asking, washing his car as reward for such an amazing performance in bed. If it is quality time, try to spend a little extra time doing something they love whether cuddling up for a movie, or just holding each other in silence. Getting them a little gift to say I love you. This does not have to be overly expensive, if financially you are strained, start by picking a rose.

Rev. David Grant said, "I have known of marriages that have ended in divorce because of poor hygiene. I am not talking about persons having medical issues and as a result, would carry an odor. I am talking about persons who refused to bathe for days at a time. Having travelled, I know this is acceptable in some cultures as it is said that body odor is used to attract the opposite sex. However, in the West where we are from, this is unacceptable and becomes a major turn-off. One divorced woman shared with me how her husband would come into the bed dirty and smelly and desiring her to give herself intimately to him. She confessed to me that she could not go through with an act of intimacy as she found the odor repulsive and would have even caused her to vomit on occasions." Taking a good bath (preferably together), sometimes that is where the intimacy will begin, right there in the shower. Nothing like the right temperature hot water aiding the intimate moments in the shower. Washing the creases, flaps, and folds, giving your spouse access to all of you. Applying fragrances to those points of the body where the pulse can be felt is yet a simple but effective way to arouse one's spouse through the sense of smell. Rev. Grant said, 'there is a particular cologne I do not wear anymore as more than one woman (my wife not included) has told me that it turns them on.' Go fragrance shopping with your spouse or while shopping try different fragrances and make a note of what excites your spouse and return and purchase. The pubic area can be another grave cause of concern. Some persons carry more hair than others. We must endeavor to dry that area properly. Trimming or shaving can also alleviate repugnant odors in that area. Invest in moisturizers or powders that will make the intimacy experience more delightful for your spouse. Another divorcee shared with me how her former husband would not want to wash his penis before sex. She had to be the one to clean him up. He would repeatedly say to her that "cows do not wash their feet, but yet it is sold." Intimacy is not about one person. It is a partnership. Do what is needed for your spouse to enjoy you. It has been psychologically proven that men are moved by what they see and women are moved by what they hear. When we look in the fashion industry, we see more revealing clothes being made for ladies than there are for men. You can find on any television network advertisements with scantily dressed women selling something like tractor tires. What does a scantily dressed attractive or rather sexually appealing woman have to do with tractor tires? Nothing more than it gives visual appeal and sends a subliminal message that you need tires and if you come and purchase here you could meet this gorgeous hot babe that you have been fantasizing about. Oh, by the way, she doesn't own or has ever driven a tractor and neither does she work there.

When you were getting married you had those sexually appealing six-pack abs. Now you are older and wiser you just pack everything in one oversized gut. We must try to maintain that which we had at the start. Science has discovered a law called, The Law of Gravity. Ladies, those beautiful, firm, perky breasts will sag after a child or two. This is natural, so you don't need to assist the process by going braless while lactating. The skin of the breast automatically stretches because of the milk being produced. Let us seek to continue to make ourselves sexually appealing so our spouse won't always be asking for the lights to be turned off on our intimate moments. Enrol in an exercise program together to tighten all these "loose" areas. There is a reality that we all must face and not try to ignore. Both partners are bombarded daily with images of the opposite sex that looks better than us. We are not and should not be in competition with those outside but let us make it easier for our spouses not to take a second look. We alluded earlier to the fact that women are moved by what they hear. If we should check the statistics we will find that more love songs are done by males. I am well aware that there are more males in the industry but in comparing the subject matter of the songs, men sing more about love-making than their counterparts. The right sentence said at the right time, in the right atmosphere, to the right person can be the fire that ignites deep intimacy. However, the converse is so true. The tone, texture, and volume of what is said could make her swing on the chandelier. I remember having a conversation with one Christian lady, who was sixty-five at the time, telling how she would put on her lingerie and dance on her dining table for her husband. Crawling over to him and whispering in his ears and how sexually aroused he would become. She looked the part and spoke the part. That is hitting the target right there. That man do not need to look at another woman. He has it all at home. The atmosphere is of great significance. The ambiance can make or break the mood. Sounds, scents, and sight all make up the intimate experience. Please understand that it does not always have to be ballads. It can be Soca, Lover's Rock, or some Afro-Cuban music. The mood you setting will determine what kind of music you would employ. Knowing your partner's taste in music is vital. Opera is not best suited for a Dance-Hall lover to achieve your desired result.

Candles, rose petals, lights dimmed low with soft music in the background have been the television imagery of romance and intimacy over the centuries. Do not limit your times of intimacy to stereotypes. Be more than willing to explore other atmospheres that could arouse your passion. Some foods are natural aphrodisiacs. Not only by taste but even the scent. I encourage you to open the doors of your mind and be creative in your expressions of intimacy. Go on that voyage of discovery, where to touch, when to touch. What to say, when to say it and how to say it. Look sexy and be sexy for your spouse and keep someone else out of your house.

Let me reiterate, it is important to note that intimacy does not stop after one have reached his or her sexual climax or orgasm. Again, it goes back to knowing your partner's body and being sexually synched with each other.

## CHAPTER 3
## THE LITTLE THINGS

It is said that we must learn to appreciate the little things. Can we truly get to a place where we appreciate the little things? Life is full of the little things, but we get so caught up in the big things we miss out on the little things that help to make our marriages more pleasant and enjoyable. Stopping to appreciate the fresh air, pausing to admire God's creation, the birds, and flowers, just to stop and smell the roses. We live in this microwave society where things are always on the go, instant, right now. This results in us missing on the little things. In appreciating the little things, it will assist you to slow down, take it is easy, be grateful and help you to be patient.

We should never allow the lack of resources like money to stop us from appreciating the little things. Let us remember that the perfect marriage does not exist. Two imperfect people are joined together to live as one. Marriage is a lot of work and requires time, patience, commitment and needs both parties involved to give all of themselves for it to work. No one formula works for all marriages, what works for the Browns might not necessarily work for the Whites.

Guidworld.com says "Most of us tend to think that it is the big things in life that make us happy and it's the big things that are the most important. However, the real truth is it is the little things that mean the most".

On the day you get married, there are major things that must be in place for the wedding to be performed. Marriage licenses must be attained, the bride and groom in their wedding attire, the person officiating the wedding and at least one witness must be present. These are just a few of the major things for this very special event in your life to take place. However, we get so enthralled in the excitement of the day we miss the little things, like enjoying your wedding, you miss your spouse blowing you a kiss across the room. It is these little things which are quite important but are easily missed.

The little things are what helps to build intimacy in a marriage whether you are newlywed or married for a long time.

A dear friend said, she remembered when she got married. It was a joyous time for her and her man. They had their families and friends celebrating the big day with them. Some of their inner circle friends stayed at the hotel with them. But that night she said they were too tired to consummate their union. The next day after, friends came knocking at their door. They enjoyed them being there but after they left, it was their quiet time and the passion was turned up all day. The sex was great but after the first orgasm, the intimacy without the penetration produced more of those orgasms. It is the little things of understanding that they were both too tired and friends were close by.

Learning to appreciate each other by simply saying Thank you. Thanking your spouse for making dinner. Having your spouse working in the kitchen especially after a long day at work or looking after the kids. Just to hear you say those two words can make a world of difference and make your spouse feel appreciated and loved. Thanking your spouse for being supportive and understanding when you are not having one of your best days. Saying thank you after making love is an indication of how much you really appreciate each other.

Complimenting your spouse is a little thing that means a lot and goes a long way. Honey, you are making that dress look good, I love how your hair looks today. Babes you smell so good today, is that a new fragrance you are wearing? I could eat you up right now. Complimenting each other helps to encourage your spouse to want to look after themselves and can also create the ambiance for the desire to pamper each other. Compliments can help to boast self-confidence especially if your spouse have issues about their body and the way how they look.

Hugging and kissing each outside of having sex are sometimes overlooked. A spouse should not only want to hug or kiss their partner only when they desire sex. Spontaneously hugging and planting a kiss on the mouth, cheeks or neck are some of the little things that can increase intimacy in a marriage. It builds anticipation and creates excitement. A wife complained that her husband does not kiss her anymore, she had to ask him if she had bad breath. Affectionately touching each other can help to demonstrate how much you value, care and is attracted to each other. Spending time alone without the kids, going out on dates having "Just us times" together are some of the little things that should not be neglected. Going for walks in the neighborhood together are times to be treasured. Making time to interact, reconnect and share, are the little things that should not be taken for granted. Alone time with each other is to be nurtured- no cell phones, friends or family.

Time together praying with each other is a major little thing that should not be missed. It really does make a difference in your relationship. Prayer is said to be the breath that gives life to any Christian home and relationship. Prayer opens your hearts to forgiveness and the ability to tolerate each other's differences. Praying together gives room for honesty and transparency. Prayer allows God to be the centre of the marriage. Prayer also brings growth and transformation. Not focusing on the negatives and shortcomings in your spouse will allow you to appreciate the little things about them. Yes, he may not help with the house chores and will never put the toilet seat down, but he takes time to pray with you and is always complimenting you, letting you know what a great mother/wife you are. She may never go to the football game with you but she ensures that you have your lunch prepared with your favorite snacks every day for work. Focusing on the brighter side and all that is good and right as the word of God says in Philippians 4:8 *"Finally, brethren, whatsoever things are true, whatsoever things are honest, whatsoever things are just, whatsoever things are pure, whatsoever things are lovely, whatsoever things are of good report; if there be any virtue, and if there be any praise, think on these things"*.

Laughter helps us to not take everything too seriously and miss the little things. It is said that "Partners who can laugh together, stay together" so don't be afraid to just be silly with your partner sometimes. Instead of getting angry and arguing, use that opportunity to see the humor in the situation. Many times, when we do so it will allow us to see what was causing you to be angry with each other. It was not that serious in the first place but was just blown out of proportion. Job 8:21 'Till he fill thy mouth with laughing, and thy lips with rejoicing" Laughter is good for the soul!

When your spouse does something thoughtful, make sure you recognize the effort even if it is not done to your liking. Sometimes it is the thought that counts. The minor annoying thing that we tend to focus on and turn them into major are what causes us to miss the little things and criticize instead of compliment. Use every opportunity given to say kind and considerate things. *"A soft answer turns away wrath: but grievous words stir up anger". Proverbs 15:1.*

Be spontaneous and do the little thing that your spouse is not expecting. On the way home from work gather a bunch of wildflowers (if money is an issue to buy flowers) surprise your wife with them just to say I missed you today and wanted to say I love you with these flowers. Surprise your husband with his favorite snack while he is relaxing. The smiles on their face in receiving this gift unexpectedly will warm your heart with love and appreciation. These are the little moments that will make your day and will not be easily forgotten.

A friend admitted that when her husband is talking to her at times even though she is there with him in his presence she is not really listening. She had mastered the art of tuning him out and this have caused her to miss hearing some very important things her husband was sharing at some very critical moment. Listening carefully about each other's day, worries, dreams and aspirations are little things that show that you care and is interested in what your spouse has to say. James 1: 19 tells us to *"Wherefore, my beloved brethren, let every man be swift to hear, slow to speak, slow to wrath"*.

Apologize with humility quickly and ask for forgiveness. There is a quote that reads *"Forgiveness is the best form of love. It takes a strong person to say sorry and an even stronger person to forgive"* It is not easy at times to admit that you are wrong, to say you are sorry and ask for forgiveness. Many marriages have been broken because one party refuses to apologize or to forgive. A simple act of saying I am sorry could have prevented a little thing from becoming a big thing.

Be a source of encouragement for your spouse with the little things. Your spouse is having a challenging time at work. One way you can encourage and motivate them is by placing little sticky notes of encouragement in their lunch bag, or on the steering wheel as the get ready to drive or sending a text just to say "I believe in you, you can do this", "I am Praying and thinking about you". Archbishop Duncan Williams says *"The greatest gift you can give a person is faith in them to know they can stand anything".*

There is a saying that says" Little is much when God is in it". Let God be the in midst of your marriage. He can turn those little things into big things that can make a huge difference in the life of your marriage. Purpose to be kind, selfless, compassionate, **submissive**, obedient, committed, joyful and most of all loving towards your spouse. There is strength in unity, be on one accord, heaven reacts to unity. Marriage is not all roses and romance all the time, there will be challenges, good and bad days. Learn to appreciate and accept the small things with so much more love and affection. After all, it is the little things that matter the most in life, and that is what makes a marriage worthwhile having.

## CHAPTER 4
## INTIMATE LANGUAGE

Readers, the error of waiting until you are in bed to begin intimacy is crazy. Someone once said, a man is like a light switch, just a flicker and he is ready but a woman is like a motor, it needs warming up. In the pursuit of fulfilling a more intimate relationship between husband and wife, a couple should study each other carefully. I call this developing and knowing your intimate language. Within every language, there are words and actions that mean the same but sometimes carry varying weight of expressions. I need you when one is not feeling well is different from I need you when sexual hormones are high. In developing your intimate language, care must be given to ensure the intended message is conveyed. A couple is in a huge gathering and they are seeing each other but are not immediately within reach of each other. Using her intimate language, the wife began expressing her desire for sexual pleasure. Please understand that your smile must carry different meanings. She smiled invitingly while she glides her fingers through her hair. She blushes and without uttering a word, she speaks to him between smiles. She stands and purposely falls her purse and then slowly picks it up while looking at her gift from God. To pick up the purse is not done by stooping down but rather a bend over. Message delivered! The husband now must not entertain his friends who desires to converse at length after the meeting is finished. His queen awaits him. Never put the needs of your partner at the file of casual.

One couple when asked about their marital intimate language said:

a) During working hours, a text message is sent saying, "thinking about you or will you be home early tonight"?
b) Whenever the wife needs sexual pleasure, she asks her husband if he is not going to shower.
c) A pic of a sexy underwear at the feet is sent by text.
d) Sometimes a straight to the point message that reads- I am horny.

The husband on the other hand says:

a) I enjoyed you last time.
b) You are like fine wine, gets better with time.
c) Are you menstruating?
d) I hate when you are on your cycle.
e) "I miss you"- although they shared the same bed a few hours ago.

Another says the wife puts her under clothes in his view before proceeding to the bathroom. The sexier they are the stronger the message. The gently slapping of the bottom as he passes her is a major hit and the seemingly accidental brush of the breast is a greatly received gesture.

Some years ago, at a marriage retreat, couples spoke about the usage of the names they coined for each other's genitalia. This was a big hit in the intimate language. Names like; Peace and Tranquillity, Stiff and Sweet, Tight and Good, Deliverer, Angle, Needle Eye and God's Gift to name a few. If you have not yet coined your partner's intimate genital name, please do so. And if you have been using the same old one, it will not hurt to develop a new one. Please note that, you can have more than one and is used depending on the mood you are in. Example, if you want an evening of romance, you might use

God's Gift but if you desire hard core sex you employ Stiff and Sweet.

## CHAPTER 5
## ERRORS OF COMPARISON

We are created, yes, in the Image and Likeness of God. But we are all unique and peculiar in our own ways. We all have different purposes and roles to play within this world and the kingdom of God. One individual can never be the same as another, nor need to be intimidated or infuriated by another. Much less be jealous and covetous of another. Especially amongst husbands and wives.

It is the enemies' plan to divide and conquer husbands and wives, and all which is birthed from a successful marriage. One of the mechanisms he uses to do so is comparison. The Webster dictionary gives us the definition of comparison to be **"similarities or dissimilarities between two things or people"**. And so as a husband or wife, it is unfair for you to compare your significant other to a former individual whom you had a prior relationship with or with whom you desire them to be and amongst yourself. Keep in mind that every individual comes from a completely different background, and does not have the same qualities of your now spouse nor is everyone's spiritual maturity on the same level.

When we are new born believers in Christ the word of God says that we are a new creation in Christ, old things have passed away (2 Corinthians 5:17). This is a new relationship/marriage, so treat it as such. God did not take nor will he use your past, being that you are new in Him to judge you. It is what you do while being saved, a new creation that will be analysed at the end of your journey. Comparison of past relationships within your marriage or comparison amongst spouses can break down the marriage tremendously. It can cause a spouse to feel unworthy and not good enough. It can cause tension, and frequent altercation wherein one is trying to keep up with the other's race, when we are all called to run our own race. This can also leave one burned out, tired and weary from trying to keep up with one's former relationship or the expectancy of their spouse. Comparison of another can also lead unto one doing that which is not of them, but to please their loved ones they will do it.

At the end of the day, making comparison of your spouse with another, can be both detrimental unto the one making the comparison and also unto he or she whom it is being spoken unto/ directed at. For you making the comparison, sheds light and speaks highly of how you feel within yourself. It also reflects and shows that which is in your heart. For what is in your heart, is within your mind and will be reflected within your action and speech. The image and likeness of the individual can be jeopardized. Mental health can be affected, and once the mental health is affected even down to the very health of that individual can be affected as well.

Imagine you being the recipient of any of the following:

a) Your baked chicken is nothing compared to my ex.
b) John knew how to handle his manhood.
c) I know you love pink, but Mary makes pink looks fabulous.

Intimate comparison can easily destroy a marriage. In 2020 a marriage ended in divorce because the wife told her husband that her boyfriend before him, was a better man than he was. As much as he loved his wife, the connection between them was severed by those piercing words. He said he felt less than a man and that took away all intimate desires for her. The damage was so severe, from that day until they were legally divorced, he had no more penal erection for her. As the Holy Spirit inspired men to write the bible, he was careful to speak about refraining from sexual activities until after marriage. If followed, it would eliminate majority of the problem of comparison. It would not prevent comparison in cases of death or divorce and remarriage. Where that directive of abstaining until marriage were forfeited, one should be extra careful to not compare the present with the past especially in a negative light.

Simone married the first love of her life and was comfortable with him. She was a virgin at marriage, but he was not. Everything she knew about intimacy, she garnered from him. One day, she and some friends had a conversation regarding sex and intimacy, and she was shocked at the things they spoke about. Majority of what they said sounded desirable but was foreign to her. This unfortunately propelled her to explore with one of her friends and it resulted in her marital union being dissolved. She compromised her marital vows because she compared her husband to her friend.

Comparison has the potential to block you from experiencing orgasms or the simplicity of marital happiness. Because of comparison, a marriage depleted to the point where the wife said, whenever her husband touched her, she feels as though she is being raped. She no longer had desire for her husband who in her calculation, did not measure up to what she knew before. She felt disappointed and desired more than what he was supplying.

Therefore, though the flesh at times would want to push you to compare your spouse with someone else, pray and call upon the Holy Spirit to empower you in not falling into that temptation nor being led by the flesh in that manner. And if you do find yourself making a comparison of your spouse, the only person you should compare your spouse with, is Christ Jesus. His ways and His words alone is what we are to use as the diagram on how we are to live and treat each other.

Prayer: Father in Jesus name I pray that each day for the empowerment and help of the Holy Spirit to lead and guide me. Help me not to draw comparison of myself with anyone nor compare my spouse unto anyone else except for that which is of your holy words in Jesus' name Amen.

# CHAPTER 6
# COMPLAINTS

If all marriages were perfect, then the need for this book would be non-existent. It is critical that a partner's complaints or dissatisfactions are given much attention. Both husbands and wives have complaints regarding intimacy.

    a) A popular complaint from husbands is, their wives do not initiate intimacy. This causes a feeling of rejection, not wanted and there is no interest. When a wife initiates intimacy, it boosts the husband's self-worth and let him know he is appreciated and desired.

    b) A popular complaint from wives is the immediate snoring after the ejaculation by their husbands. This seems to be almost universal. According to health experts, in the article Decoded: Why men fall asleep after sex?

*"As soon as a man reaches orgasm, his body chemistry changes. This happens when the biochemical prolactin is released, it makes him tired and he tends to sleep after an intimate session. Sex makes you feel relaxed and releases hormone oxytocin. This hormone helps in vanishing anxiety and stressful thoughts and makes it easier for you to sleep afterwards."*

The odds are against the men in this area, therefore extra intentional pursuit of not falling asleep immediately after ejaculation will be required.

c) Another complaint is the lack of cuddling after ejaculation. This will be addressed in a subsequent chapter.

d) Another popular complaint is, Christian partner gives more attention to the church than their spouse. Please, your first place of ministry is your family. Bishop Laird once told me, a happy wife a happy life. No partner must feel as though they are second to the ministry.

e) Dressing (unattractive) during dating and courting, one's outward appearance was given much attention. However, after marriage, persons have complaint that there has been a significant reduction in the beauty of the appearance department. Worn and tattered clothing at home seems to be the new norm. Some husbands have complaint about the oversized panties citing that they miss the G-strings and other sexy underwear's.

f) Unfortunately, sexual boredom and limited sexual positions was a popular complaint. One wife said it was a predicted routine. We will speak about sex positions in a subsequent chapter.

g) The refusal to try different or new things is a complaint echoed from both husbands and wives.

h) Some spouses have refrained from continuing the practise of oral sex with the complaint being it leaves their mouth smelling awful. I suggest before you make such a decision, both partners research as to the cause and how it can be eliminated.

i) As I did my research for this book, a pastor questioned his wife about any intimate complaints she has against him. She said insufficient foreplay and kissing. He was stunned as he thought he was at the top of his game in satisfying her. I challenge you to do the same with your partner.

Please do not be offended by the responses but rather get better by the critique. In my book, Mind Renewal Biblical Secrets to a Better You, I wrote, "critique me until I am my best me".

REV. LEOSTONE MORRISON

# LOVE AGAIN

Complaints are repeatedly heard from persons who have suffered pain from past relationships or because of persons they were not intimately involved with. Unfortunately, many persons are the victim of marital hurts that are beyond measure. Some have been physically, emotionally, and financially abused while others are hurting because of a divorce, death of a partner or the wicked act of rape. To protect themselves from further misuse, they have walled themselves into rooms of love isolation. They have vowed to never love again. This however can be a grave mistake and a self-imposed deprivation of the best that God has prepared for you. I encourage you to love again. In the account of Jesus and the Samaritan woman of John 4:16, we see the following conversation.

*"Jesus saith unto her, Go, call thy husband, and come hither. The woman answered and said, I have no husband. Jesus said unto her, Thou hast well said, I have no husband: For thou hast had five husbands; and he whom thou now hast is not thy husband: in that saidst thou truly."*

I have heard different messages preached that the Samaritan woman was a lady of the night, a prostitute, among others but I do not see that in scripture. What I see is a woman who believed in the institution of marriage. We do not know the circumstances that led to her having gotten married five (5) times, but we do know, those were legally binding relationships. Jesus acknowledged those unions as she having had husbands. After the fifth husband; she entered a relationship that was not legally binding. Having tried marriage, now broken with singleness, she tries another avenue.

Jesus said to her, *"the one you have now is not your husband."* She believed in marriage. We do not know if she was good at it or not, but she kept trying to be. She did not quit at the first, second or fourth time. The possibility of her husbands died leaving her is not foreign or that they divorced her for another. Truth is we do not know. We know she desired companionship and chose to do it the proper way.

In chapter 4:19-30, the woman saith unto Jesus, Sir, I perceive that thou art a prophet. The woman then left her water pot, and went her way into the city, and saith to the men, Come, see a man, which told me all things that ever I did: is not this the Christ? Then they went out of the city and came unto him.

The broken Samaritan woman was not intercepted by Jesus when she was in her marital unions but when she had a man. She experienced an encounter with the Messiah. She was convicted, converted and released to evangelize. The broken, failed at marriage, having an illegal man, the Samaritan woman was used by God to evangelize. Please note, she went to the well at an hour where the sun was very high. Persons did not go to the well at that time. But it may be, she was avoiding her peers because of her marital failures. Now with a newfound love, the same woman who was avoiding persons ran to tell people. Reader, when you come into contact with God, the things you feared, you will now face. Please be encouraged to love again, only continue searching for it the godly way.

## LOVE AFTER DEATH

Love is possible after the death of one's spouse. Death does not equate you giving up on love. In the account of 1 Samuel chapter 25, we see the death of Nabal, Abigail's husband. Verse 40-42 reads, *"His servants went to Carmel and said to*

*Abigail, "David has sent us to you to take you to become his wife.* "She bowed down with her face to the ground and said, *"I am your servant and am ready to serve you and wash the feet of my lord's servants."* Abigail quickly got on a donkey and attended by her five female servants, went with David's messengers and became his wife. Ruth also in the book of Ruth loved again and Marry Boaz after the death of her husband Mahlon. You can love again.

## RAPED

Many women have been raped and some after many years, still re-live that horrible day. I implore you to not allow the wrongs done to you to prevent you from loving again. A friend of mine was raped by her then boyfriend because he refused to wait until marriage for intimacy. She fought through the struggle and overcame. Today she is married to a pastor with children. She decided to love again.

## **DIVORCED**

I was married and that marriage failed. I remember asking God based on the teaching I received from the local church I attended, the fairness of being alone on the wrongness of my former wife. The doctrine was divorce and remarriage is a sin. No minister of the gospel must be married more than once, except the cause be death of a spouse. One day I was pointed to a portion of scripture in the book of 1 Corinthians chapter 7:27-28b, "Are you pledged to a woman? Do not seek to be released. Are you free from such a commitment? Do not look for a wife. But if you do marry, you have not sinned; and if a virgin marries, she has not sinned."

In simple words, if you are married, seek not to be divorced, if you are divorced seek not to be married. But if you marry, you have not sinned. Reader, you can love again.

Complain no more about the pain you incurred, whatever the root cause you can be intimate again.

## CHAPTER 7
## "IS IT REALLY A SIN?"

In the daily affairs of the permitted marriage between one man and one woman resides some intimate areas that many are divided on. Is it really a sin to express your love for your spouse through oral, anal sex and sexual beatings?

There is no clear scripture that says either of the three are wrong or right. If there is, I missed it. We see thou shalt not kill, but thou shalt not beat, do oral nor anal sex to your marital partner is missing. I know we are looking at it from within the marriage setting but let us step back a bit to outside of that marital union.

In the book of Ephesians chapter 5:3 declares, "But among you there must not be even a hint of sexual immorality, or of any kind of impurity ...because these are improper for God's holy people." The biblical definition of "immorality" is *"any form of sexual contact outside of marriage"* (1 Corinthians 7:2). According to the Bible, sex is to be reserved for marriage (Hebrews 13:4). Therefore, yes, oral, anal sex and sexual beatings is a sin if done before or outside of marriage

We see another scripture which promotes intimacy within the marital union. 1 Corinthians 7:2 states, *"Nevertheless, because of sexual immorality, let each man have his own wife, and let each woman have her own husband."* And Hebrews 13:4, states, *"Marriage is honorable among all, and the bed undefiled; but fornicators and adulterers God will judge."*

With that established, let us go back now to the marriage setting.

## ORAL SEX

Shortly after I got saved, I asked the senior pastor about the wrong or right of oral sex within the Christian marriage, and he told me Hebrew 13:4.

He said the pastor has no say within the bedroom of a couple. Within every marital sexual encounter, there are three entities present and the pastor is not one. Marriage consists of the husband, wife and God.

As said before the Bible says the marriage is honorable and the bed undefiled. What does honorable and undefiled mean? Honorable means pleasing and undefiled means clean. I found the following article from Got Questions;

Is oral sex a sin if done within a marriage?

*Many, perhaps most, Christian married couples have had this question. What makes it difficult is the fact that the Bible nowhere says what is allowed or disallowed sexually between a husband and wife, other than, of course, any sexual activity that involves another person (swapping, threesomes, etc.) or that involves lusting after another person (pornography). Outside of these two restrictions, the principle of "mutual consent" would seem to apply (1 Corinthians 7:5). While this text specifically deals with abstaining from sex/frequency of sex, "mutual consent" is a good concept to apply universally in regard to sex within marriage. Whatever is done, it should be fully agreed on between the husband and his wife. Neither spouse should be forced or coerced into doing something he/she is not completely comfortable with. If oral sex is done within the confines of marriage and in the spirit of mutual consent, there is not a biblical case for declaring it to be a sin.*

Clifford and Joyce Penner, in their book *The Gift of Sex*, give this definition of oral sex: "Oral sex or oral stimulation is the stimulation of your partner's genitals with your mouth, lips, and tongue. The man may stimulate the woman's clitoris and the opening of the vagina with his tongue, or the woman may pleasure the man's penis with her mouth." This sexual stimulation may or may not lead to orgasm for the husband and wife. The husband is often thought to be the recipient of oral sex and wife the giver. The assumption is that the husband is more desirous to have it done vs the wife. But the truth be told the wife is just as keen of having oral sex performed on her. Oral sex is a great way for both husband and wife to pleasure each other. Intercourse alone does not provide enough pleasure for orgasm for most women. Therefore, the need for manual/oral stimulation is essential.

A good advice regarding oral sex is to practice good hygiene and keep your genital nice and clean. Be considerate of your partner and what he or she is comfortable with. If you want them to dine, it is up to you to make oral as appetizing as possible. Get creative with positions - mix up your oral game by physically moving around and trying new positions, just like you do in the rest of your sex life. Make it fun. Sex is a gift from God and should be treated and enjoyed as such. God wants you to enjoy this gift.

## IS ANAL SEX REALLY WRONG?

Anal sex between a husband and a wife is not mentioned in the bible. In Genesis 19, male angels went to Sodom and the homosexual minded men desired to have sexual intercourse with them. But that is different. That is man to man which is clearly defined by the Bible as being wrong.

The word Sodomy which comes from the word Sodom has taken on a modern meaning which is any penetration anally. However, in biblical terminology, sodomy would be man to man. Some persons will run to the following text, Romans 1:26-27 to prove the wrongness of anal sex.

*For this reason God gave them up to vile passions. For even their women exchanged the natural use for what is against nature. 27 Likewise also the men, leaving the natural use of the woman, burned in their lust for one another, men with men committing what is shameful, and receiving in themselves the penalty of their error which was due.*

Notice, men left the natural use of the woman and went to man- homosexuality not anal sex.

Although it can be deduced that the same principle that governs oral sex within a marriage governs anal sex within the marriage also, there are medical implications that should not be ignored. The following is an excerpt from a Newsletter of Medical News Today.

*The anus lacks the cells that create the natural lubricant the vagina has. It also does not have the saliva of the mouth. The rectum's lining is also thinner than that of the vagina. Lack of lubrication and thinner tissues increase the risk of friction-related tears in the anus and rectum. Some of these tears may be very small, but they still expose the skin. Because stool that naturally contains bacteria passes through the rectum and anus when leaving the body, the bacteria can potentially invade the skin through these tears. This increases the risk of anal abscesses, a deep skin infection that usually requires treatment with antibiotics.*

## SEXUAL BEATINGS

Years ago, I met a couple who expressed their undying love for each other through beatings. Whenever the female desired a good love making, she would aggravate the male into a wrath until he started to beat her. Recently a young man asked my advice in a relationship. His partner desired him to kick, thump and box her repeatedly during intimacy. There are some young ladies that are of the position, if he does not beat me he does not love me. They understand beating as a high demonstration of love. Should she be frowned on because that is her desire? Do we have the right to dictate to persons what they should desire from their partner?

Is there any scripture that says beatings within the marriage is wrong?

As you search the scriptures, you see Ephesians 5:25 which states, *"Husbands, love your wives, as Christ loved the church and gave himself up for her."*

Often within Christendom, you hear persons say, "Jesus or the Holy Spirit is beating someone who messed up." If that is true, should the husband beat his wife if she messes up? God scolds us but He does it in love with the aim of making us better and not for us to fear Him, not for us to not want to come to Him. Not for us to no longer have a relationship with Him. When a man beat his wife is it in line with loving her like how God loves the church? Women should be submissive allowing the men to be the head of the household. Does this submission include sexual beatings? What about the reverse, where the wife beats the man, is this in line with what God called women to do?

Outside of beating as we know it, there are couples who practice autoerotic asphyxia (choking). This is where one partner chokes the neck of his/her partner during intimacy. This sounds scary.

Someone once put forth the following: In the book of Esther, queen Vashti dishonored her husband and was removed as being queen. This was a permanent decision. She was stripped of royalty, prestige, and influence. Would it not have been easier that she be beaten by her husband for an hour? Her pain would have been eased and she would retain her position. Certain things may not be directly said in scripture however, I believe we can align it to what the Bible says to make a difference. Hearing of persons who desire sexual beatings have earned responses like, they need help and they enjoy being beaten is a sign of emotional trauma or self-esteem issues. If they have consented and is enjoying their sexual escapades, are we in a position to judge their private actions as being wrong?

Disclaimer- I have not put forward my personal beliefs. I am merely inviting you to have discussions with your partner as you continue the pursuit of improved marital intimacy.

## CHAPTER 8
## SEX TOYS

*A*re sex toys within a marriage between two consenting adults advised or are they sinful? Is it not the responsibility of a husband and wife to spice up their sexual relationship as they feel best?

A wife said the following to me (I have permission to share), "My masturbation door was opened through my husband, therefore I thought it was something good. He bought me my first vibrator but after a while, my interest in sexual intimacy with him was almost completely depleted. All I wanted was the vibrator. I was so addicted to the vibrator that no battery could stay in the remotes at home."

Her husband was not experiencing erectile dysfunction but thought it a good addition to their sex life as they discussed adding extra spice to their marriage. He eventually terminated the rights of occupancy to the vibrators he bought as he realized he was losing miserably to machines and his wife desired the vibrator more than him. No matter how skilful a sex partner believe they are, there is a moment of climaxing or peaking. There are husbands who have abandoned their wives for mannequins. They are making them now with vibrating vagina, body heat and vaginal liquid. Machines will outlive you as long as the power from the battery keeps flowing.

They both underestimated the effect the toy would have on her and their marriage. The vibrator became the third person in the marriage, which by God's standard is a marital violation. It took the place of the husband, and no one wants to feel replaced. A marriage is between two, not three.

While it is encouraged to continually be sprucing up your marriage, caution must be employed as this is pursued. You have to be careful with what you allow in the bedroom. You do not want to give the enemy an open invitation to your lives.

My friend said, after she reconnected with the Lord, she found out it was wrong, but the habit was not easily broken. She failed many times but kept praying and repenting for deliverance.

## SEXUAL AID

What if the scenario shifted slightly to rather than a vibrator being introduced as a medium of intimate spice, but rather it was because of erectile dysfunction? Erectile dysfunction is a condition where a man cannot get or keep an erection firm enough for sexual intercourse. According to James 5:14-15, *"Is anyone among you sick? Let them call for the elders of the church to come and pray over you, anointing you with oil in the name of the Lord. And the prayer of faith will save him who is sick, and the Lord will restore him."* Yes I believe in the resurrection power of Jesus. However, in this scenario, who should anoint and lay hands? Should the elders of the church anoint the malfunctioning penis with oil while they pray or should the wife be the one to anoint? If God chooses not to restore the dysfunctioning penis, can that couple introduce a vibrator to assist? Before you hurry to respond, please allow me to make that decision a little harder.

As knowledge increases, aid have been developed which have become the deliverer to many who were in dire need. For those with deformity of the legs and arms, the prosthesis foot and arms have been created. We see men and women daily living complete lives thanks to this aid. If a marriage is suffering from erectile dysfunction, should a vibrator which is an aid not be utilized? Are we hypocrites in sanctioning the artificial leg and arm while rejecting the artificial penis? As a young minister, I was confronted by a discouraged, ready to get a divorce wife, because her husband was the victim of erectile dysfunction. They had tried medical, herbal, and spiritual solutions but to no avail. She asked if they could introduce artificial penis. I was not sure how to respond, therefore I asked for time to consult a senior pastor. I was advised that they could with conditions.

1. Both husband and wife must agree to the aid
2. Both must decide on the color and size of the aid. This is primarily in ensuring that the aid purchased resembles in size and color as much as possible that of the husband.
3. The usage of the aid must only be implemented when both partners are present.

## CHAPTER 9
## DIVINE PLEASURE

I was not always a Christian and was not a virgin when I got married. With that said, please permit me to share with you the myths I learned as a young man with regards to being a good intimate sex partner. I thought that the degree of your effectiveness was directly related to the amount of pain and noise that your partner makes. Love making was defined by roughness and pain. One older male said, you should ensure that you have a needle or pin with you. If the female is not making any noise, you should gently prick her. This has led to a monster in many marriages- deception. The faking of pleasure and climax has continued to be a sore that needs immediate healing. My friend Donna said, "You must first break the ego so that the male can be helped."

Some years ago, a friend said to me, sexual intercourse is a race- who cum (climaxed) first wins. I thought he was just being funny until he proceeded to explain that, each person was responsible for their climaxing or ejaculation. This is a terrible myth that unfortunately is one of the main reasons for the dissatisfaction of many wives. The Bible tells us in Philippians 2:3-4,

*"Do nothing out of selfish ambition or vain conceit, but in humility consider others better than yourselves. Each of you should look not only to your own interests, but also the interests of others."*

Selfishness or self-pleasing must never be allowed to escape suffocation in marital intimacy. A dear friend said, he and his wife were having intercourse and he lost consciousness of her fulfilment and was enjoying himself to the point of almost climaxing when his wife shouted repeatedly- send it, back send it back. She recognized that he had gone left her and she was not near climaxing. He had to delay his landing until she too was ready to land also. That is not the easiest thing to do, however it is possible. Many persons might not consider this feasible or necessary; but praying asking God to teach you how to satisfy your partner is still a powerful exercise in sexual intimacy. One husband said, he perceived that he was not satisfying his wife and went into prayer. He asked God who designed the body and sex for help, and God came through mightily for them. It is God's will that intimacy in marriage is not lame, boring or unfulfilling. The truth is, the male is the more likely partner to climax first. If this happens, it is the husband's responsibility, his mandate to ensure that his wife climaxes. There are several avenues that can be pursued to this end.

1. After ejaculation, the wife can caress her penis back to hardness.

2. She can choose to do oral sex on her husband taking him back to hardness.
3. The husband can do oral sex on his wife until she climaxes
4. He can use his fingers to caress her clitoris until she climaxes.

It is extremely unfair and should be considered illegal for one partner to be left hanging. Please consider the trauma of entering sexual intimacy knowing that, you are setting yourself up for another disappointment. This is probably one of the main reasons she seems uninterested in sexual intimacy. Husbands, the more you please your wife, the more she will desire to be intimate with you.

## COMMERCIAL SEX

An unsaved male friend of mine told me when he wants a good sex, he finds himself a sex worker, but not any sex worker. He has a special lady. The very first time he had sex with her that was it. He was hooked but only to her. Yet, he had his good darling sweet wife at home. My question is, what is missing at home? Before you scorn and crucify the sex worker, is there anything a wife can learn from her? They, the sex workers, seem to know how to make things happen in the rental bedroom. Is it plain hard-core sex that brings pleasure to a starving soul or is it a combination of hard-core and intimacy at a high level? Whichever is the case, something is missing from the marital bed. So, is commercial sex more appealing?

Let us take a keen look into these commercial sex escapades. After the one-night stand of commercial sex, how do you perform with your wife? Because there are certain acts performed with the sex worker, in the rental bedroom, to which the wife may be uncomfortable or maybe unorthodox to. What do you do to navigate the intricacies of soft sex to hard-core sex in order to make it more appealing? There is no guarantee that one partner may not step out. However, it is advised that the sex in the marital bedroom must be so good that even if he steps out in the rental bedroom with the sex worker, the sex in the marital bedroom must win.

What can be learnt from commercial sex?

Sex workers earn their living by having sexual intercourse with various partners. The more customers one gets, the more financially rewarding the trade is. For her to maintain her customer base, she must ensure that her vagina remains in excellent condition. She must never allow the wear and tear to become the status of her product. Hence, she employs certain exercises that are good for the rebuilding and tightening of the vaginal muscles. Therefore, the first lesson to be learnt from a sex worker is, do exercises that are conducive to the tightening of one's vagina. In an article written by *"How to Kegel"* BY KRISTEN J GOUGH we see the following;

> *"Kegel exercises are designed to tone your pelvic floor muscles. Unlike your abdominal muscles or your biceps, you can't see these muscles. They're deep inside your pelvis, stretching from your spine to your pubic bone, and they keep your bladder, uterus and rectum in place. They also help control the opening and closing mechanisms within your urethra, the tube through which urine leaves your body."*

The sex worker knows to build her clientele; she must place emphasis on pleasing her guests. She is therefore to live the slogan; "your wish is my command". If the client requires her to bark like a dog, dance or dress like a nurse, his will she fulfils. In the book of Esther, we see where the king made a request of his wife, and she failed to fulfil it and that cost her the queenship. She lost her crown and her position. Many husbands and wives complain that their desires are not being fulfilled. Wives, there is a word most people do not like, maybe they do not understand the meaning and what it entails. That word is *compromise.* There should be a compromise in the bedroom agreeable to both parties. If you want your spice and cinnamon in your bedroom you have to compromise or dissatisfaction will dominate.

Conversely, women, how many times have you had sex with your man and left unsatisfied? Do you know what orgasm is? Have you ever experienced that ecstasy as one entering a realm you have never entered before and a desire to remain? Wives, that realm consist of levels that intimacy will take you and penal penetration has not even happen yet.

If the answer is yes, surrender everything to that man. If the answer is no, then you need to ask yourself some serious questions. Are you expecting more than what your man can give? Do you talk to your partner while having sex or do you need to explore various sex positions- for more on sex positions see chapter ten. Some men ejaculate quickly for various reasons. Let us look a little closer on ejaculation.

## EJACULATION/CLIMAX

Sexual pursuits generally have four stages: craving, stimulation, erection, and ejaculation. An everyday name for ejaculation is cum. When the husband ejaculates, he releases semen which is a pasty white fluid that contains sperms. According to an article written by Chimene Richa, MD Potential problems with ejaculation include:

- *Premature ejaculation (PE): Ejaculating earlier during sex than you or your partner intended. This condition affects a third of men aged 18 to 59. Fortunately, the American*

*Urological Association reports that 95% of cases improve with treatment (AUA, n.d.). PE is thought to be caused by a combination of psychological and biological factors, and treatment is via behavioral and medical therapies.*

- *Delayed ejaculation: Ejaculation that takes longer than you (or your partner) would like is among the least understood and least common, less than 3% of men, male sexual dysfunction (Althof, 2016). Some men may need more than 20-25 minutes of stimulation to reach orgasm and ejaculate. Difficulty achieving ejaculation can sometimes result from depression, anxiety, alcohol use, medication use, or diabetes; addressing these issues may improve ejaculation.*

- *Retrograde ejaculation: Sometimes referred to as a "dry orgasm," retrograde ejaculation happens when the semen travels backward into the bladder rather than out of the penis. Men with this condition are still able to orgasm but without the accompanying ejaculation. In retrograde ejaculation, you might notice that your urine looks cloudy because of the semen mixed in, especially if you urinate right after sex. Common causes include prostate surgery, specifically transurethral resection of the prostate (TURP), bladder surgery, and diabetes.*

Excitement can be a major factor in quick ejaculation. One husband said, the reason he does not do much foreplay before penal penetration is because foreplay increases his excitement and that causes him to climax quickly. He said in pursuit of not ejaculating before his wife climaxes, he opted to cuddling after ejaculation. While that is thoughtful and must be applauded, he could communicate this truth with his wife and sometimes, come to an ejaculation during foreplay then do penal penetration.

Another factor can be starvation. The sexually starved husband, especially for a long period of time, might need divine intervention to not ejaculate quickly when sex is finally received. Please allow me to warn wives and husband biblically about sex starving (locking of shop).

*The husband should give to his wife her conjugal rights, and likewise the wife to her husband. For the wife does not have authority over her own body, but the husband does. Likewise, the husband does not have authority over his own body, but the wife does. Do not deprive one another, except perhaps by agreement for a limited time, that you may devote yourselves to prayer; but then come together again, so that Satan may not tempt you because of your lack of self-control. (1 Corinthians 7:3-5)*

Please read that again. Let me help you read it, "Do not deprive one another except by agreement". This means a husband, or a wife should not decide to go on fasting without the consent or approval of their partner.

Climax is the most intense, exciting, or important point of something, a culmination or apex. Yet some women unfortunately have not experienced the glory of climax. Why is this? Let us briefly discuss factors why these women have not experienced the culmination of intimacy through orgasms and or sexual intercourse. There are medical reasons which include:

a) Hormonal changes (menopause).
b) Medication.
c) Childbirth.

But there are other factors why women do not experience orgasm in intimacy. Selfishness on the part of her spouse. Pleasure and satisfaction are all about him; premature ejaculation, consistent masturbation, fear of not being able to satisfy, flaccid penis (no erection), and age.

But there is hope and help for both parties if they genuinely desire not flickering but sizzling flames in the bedroom. This book was written for that very reason. To inform, teach, and edify by decreasing the frustration and lack of pleasure in the bedroom. To ensure a decrease in divorces in the church.

## CHAPTER 10
## WORK OF ART

During sexual intercourse, the pressure of maintaining an erection is solely on the husband. For this to be achieved until the wife climaxes can be challenging at times. It takes art to refrain from ejaculating and also prepare one's wife to have an orgasm. The male can therefore employ various strategies that will help in having a pleasurable time together, where both partners are satisfied.

a) Study yourself and your partner. Every person has at least one sexual position that increases and decreases the rate of their climax. A quickie will not see the slow rate position being utilized nor will a marathon be facilitated by the fast rate of climax position.

b) During an act of penal penetration, a husband who had sought the Lord for sexual help, heard the Holy Spirit said, "Change your position". He obeyed and immediately, the ejaculation that was boiling and about to explode, was delayed until the wife climaxed. Please practice a rhythmic changing of positions. It is said that variety is the spice of life.

c) The scripture according to Proverbs 23:7a states, *"for as he thinketh in his heart, so is he."* The power of creative thinking is a powerful asset in marital intimacy. The husband can take his mind to a very cool place which if done properly, will reduce the heat and sexual rush, resulting in a longer performance. A place like inside a refrigerator, probably eating ice or swimming in very cold water. The trick to this is not to stay there too long. That can have a negative effect.

d) To promote climaxing, one wife shared that while her husband is stroking her, she caresses her clitoris. This she says stimulates her intensely and promotes quick climaxing. She explained that it is a partnership, and it is unfair to leave all the responsibility upon him.

e) One couple said they realized that after a substantial amount of foreplay before insertion, the husband ejaculates quickly. Therefore, they exchanged pre-foreplay for after ejaculation cuddling. As a couple, you must decide on what works best for you.

f) Mary said, while her husband is doing oral sex to her, he uses his finger to caress her g-spot. She explained that it is nerve wrecking. It is as though she cannot contain herself. Couples, if you have never tried this, I believe it is worth a try.

g) One says his secret is having a worship session internally to God. While he is pleasuring his wife, he is thanking and praising God. This he says makes it more intimate. He connects not only physically but spiritually.

h) A major nature killer is disrespect from a wife to her husband. Wives honor your husband. This stimulates greater performance.

i) Some wives experience vaginal dryness during pre-menopause. This can be the cause of much pain and dissatisfaction during intercourse. A quick solution is the usage of lubrication. K-Y Gel works well, or oral sex before and during penetration.

j) For some women, as they go through pre-menopause, rather than being excessively hot and moody, they experience an increase in sexual desire. It is critical that communication and understanding be utilized in this sensitive matter. Husbands must be educated as to why the sudden increase in desire for intimacy.

k) As you pursue improved marital intimacy, try new things. Not because the Bible says the bedroom is undefiled, does not mean that you should only have sexual intimacy in the bed. You can be intimate with your partner, wherever both of you agree. Only ensure that it is not in an illegal or vulgar setting. For example car, beach. This is where you get to fulfil some fantasies. Not because you are now saved, you should give up on wanting to have sex in a plane at 37000 ft. in the air.

l) Re-route your mind. This is a powerful tool. Put your mind into the sexual intimacy. Let not intimacy be only in the physical realm but also the emotional. One wife said, her husband was being intimate with her, but her mind was not involved, which resulted in her not being satisfied. There is a song that says, "My body is here but my mind is on the other side of town." This is a pleasure killer.

m) You do not need to turn off the lights; you should practice talking to each other during intimacy. Say things like, you feel good, every time you are in me, I am reminded of God's love for me, speak in tongues or just cry in joy. One wife said they were having sex and as she thought about all the unsatisfied sexual encounters she had in past relationships, she just started crying. She was blessed and was not afraid to make it known. When your partner has hit a very intense spot, say "stay right their baby". Cheer on your partner with words and actions of affirmation.

n) Do not ignore marital issues. Paul the apostle said, in 1 Corinthians 7:28, "But if you do marry, you have not sinned; and if a virgin marries, she has not sinned. But those who marry will face many troubles in this life, and I want to spare you this. "Marital Issues external to the bedroom can lead to un-pleasurable intimacy or none. Address all matters of concern, this is healthy practice.

o) Exercise. When we look at the track and field athletes running, the more they train and exercise, the better they are likely to perform. Never underestimate the wealth of exercise. This can be stimulating especially if both partners do it together. It is also a source of bonding.

## CHAPTER 11
## SEX POSITIONS

Biblically, there are two passages that speaks to laying during sexual intercourse, 2 Samuel 12:24 Genesis 39:10 (NASB) then God left sexual positons to our imagination and creativity. Some may argue that it should be confined to laying positions, yet they drive cars and take aeroplanes. I believe that is a powerful way of God demonstrating His love for us. He did not want sex to be routine and littered with rules, so like salvation, He made sexual positions free choice. There are so many comfortable sexual positions a man and his wife can participate in to make sex enjoyable and maddeningly fulfilling. It is exciting when both partners have that sexual connection in the bedroom. Each enjoying the pleasure each is giving and receiving.

Let us review some of these intimate addresses. I call them addresses because these "intimates" are not permanent. There is always room for adapting. In this chapter I purpose to show you some positions that you can introduce as you continue to improve sexual intimacy within the confines of your marriage.

The list here does not exhaust the possibilities, therefore spice up your experiences with your own "addresses".

**From the Back**

**Fig 1**

The wife kneels on over the edge where you both decide to have sex. The husband in a standing position behind her, enters paradise.

**Easy Ride**

**Fig 2**

This is similar to Reverse Cowgirl. While lying on his back, the husband raises one of his thighs. The wife sits on him and hold on to his knee while she rocks their world.

MARITAL INTIMACY

**Figures 3 through to 21 is left without names for you to make names unique to you.**

Fig 3

Fig 4

**Fig 5**

**Fig 6**

# MARITAL INTIMACY

**Fig 7**

**Fig 8**

**Fig 9**

**Fig 10**

MARITAL INTIMACY

**Fig 11**

**Fig 12**

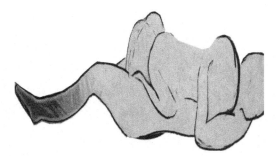

**Fig 13**

**Fig 14**

# MARITAL INTIMACY

**Fig 15**

**Fig 16**

**Fig 17**

**Fig 18**

# MARITAL INTIMACY

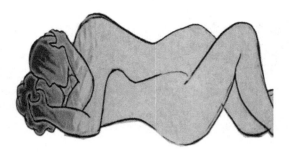

**Fig 19**

**Fig 20**

**Fig 21**

# CHAPTER 12
# GAME TIME

Marital intimacy should never be allowed to become boring or predictable. You re not to mature to play games. Some games are for children while others are for adults and some are for married couples. Here are a few for married couples.

**KISSING**

Plan or stumble into a movie time together. Then select a random word, one that you think you will hear during the duration of the movie. Each time the word is heard from the characters of the film, you kiss each other passionately. The movie is not the essence of your time together, so if you do not get to complete watching it, that is ok.

## DREAMS

Sexual dreams or fantasies should not be allowed to go unfulfilled, especially in a marriage.

Get, relatively small pieces of paper. Each piece should be big enough for the writing of one fantasy. Get a bag and deposit each partner's fantasy. You can start with three each. Shake the bag in an attempt to mix the pieces of papers. One spouse selects one. If you select one of yours, it is deposited back in the bag and the other partner gets to choose. Please ensure that the written fantasies are intimate in nature. This, although not limited to, can range from sex at a new location, new position etc. Whatever is picked from the bag that is what must be done. You do not have to rush to complete the list; you can do a three- or five-day marathon. Have fun.

## BALLOON

While listening to soft music, both husband and wife strips completely naked. Blow up a balloon or two. Place the inflated balloon on the ground between you both. Without the use of your hands, use all other body parts to transport the balloon from the ground up to your necks.

## NUMBERS

Are you in for a good time together, if yes, the numbers game is yours to play? You need two small bags and fourteen pieces of paper, seven for each of you. Each person assigns `numbers to your different body parts and make a note of it. Write numbers from one to seven on each piece of the paper, fold, and put the paper pieces in the bags.

Make your partner choose a paper piece from your bag and whatever be the number, your partner needs to fondle that particular body part. Be in no rush, this must be fun

The objective of numbers is to promote increase foreplay in your marriage. Numbers ends when all the papers have been removed from the bags. This might take more than one day. If it continues to another day, do not break days.

## MASSAGE

Life as it is can be stressing at times and a good massage maybe the answer to your partner's tension. You might not know how to give an excellent one, and that is ok. Both of you can decide to learn how to massage each other and make this a part of your intimate profile. Each person tries to outdo each other.

## PRETENSE

Plan an evening out. You arrive at the planned destination not together and pretend to be strangers. The designated person must then pursue the other partner as though it is the first time they are meeting.

## ALARM

Many persons utilize the aid of an alarm to wake them. Be your partner's alarm. Let your husband/wife be awaken by the feel of your body parts. This might be a tongue meeting the clit or a hand stroking his/her genital. Be creative, his/her body is yours. See whose alarm is more creative and pleasing.

## YOUR WISH IS MY COMMAND

Role play has been successfully used in various arenas with great success and can be fruitful in marital intimacy. Your partner is the king or queen, and you are the subject. Whatever the wish is from your king or queen, it becomes your command to carry out. (Establish boundaries before proceeding) if you have any.

## ORGASM WITHOUT PENAL PENETRATION

Can you take your partner to an orgasm without Penal Penetration? If yes, this is your time to proof it. If no, this is your time to learn how to.

## SEX CLOCK

**Fig 1**

The clock has twelve hours on it. Each hour has a different position. You can do this game either of two ways. Whatever the time of the day, you both decide to be sexually intimate, the position on the clock for that hour, is the starter. Or you could role dices, and the number that is rolled, is the position to start with or done for the duration. It is all up to you.

## TONGUE- THE MASTER KEY

After a nice shower, whether individually or together, an evening for the master key to perform is a desire. Each person has sensitive body spots that if discovered can increase pleasure and fulfillment. After a series of kissing, lay your naked partner on his or her stomach and use your tongue to navigate from right above the bottom. Gently glide your tongue along the spinal cord until you arrive at the back of his or her head (neck). Do not be in a rush to arrive at the neck, remember you are in discovery mode. Please pay attention and take mental notes of the spots that your received intimate reaction or responses to. Now at the neck, use your tongue to caress. Not by slurping but rather a tease. Nibble on the outer section of the ear and then gently use your tongue to discover within. Do not overdo, even if you are getting good responses. Return to where you started and instead of going up the spinal cord, go to the side. Most persons are sensitive to their sides, pay keen attention to the extra sensitive spots. Spend a little time here and then shift your body until your tongue hovers over your partner's foot calf. Lick your way up shifting slightly until you are at the inner thigh. You should get very good responses. Go as close to the genital area without connecting. You are not about to do oral sex. Return to the side and slowly roll your partner over unto his or her back.

Husbands do not rush to the breast or lips. Start at the navel or immediately below the navel. You are still discovering your partner's sensitive spots. Husbands, you can explore until you get very close to her breast and then swiftly go to her inner thighs. This is powerful in getting her to want you more. At this point, you can introduce cube ice. With small cubes of ice, return to the areas that you got the greatest of responses before and redo the steps.

By now you have gotten the gist of the *Tongue- the Master Key*. Please expand on what I have written here. Enjoy each other.

## CONCLUSION

There are too many unhappy marriages and while you pray, you must act also. Faith without works is still dead. God designed intimacy and expects you to enjoy it completely within the confines of marriage. The fact that you are married says you are legal to partake of the gift of God. Intimacy with your spouse is worship unto God, therefore please do not deprive God of worship. You can still have the best of your marriage if you intentionally pursue marital intimacy. It is not too late. I look forward to reading your book as you write about the changes you have made in improving your marital intimacy.

## ABOUT THE AUTHOR

Jamaican born, Rev. Leostone Peron Morrison, is the author of the book, Mind Renewal: Biblical Secrets to a Better You and the three part Mind Renewal Devotional Series among other books. He has served as an Assistant Pastor and Guidance Counselor at the Ministry of Education in Jamaica. He served as Probation Officer in the federation of Saint Kitts and Nevis.

Rev. Morrison is the founder of Restoration of the Breach without Borders Ministry, of which,

Restoration of the Breach School, hosted on the Thinkific platform, is a subsidiary. He is the founder of Next Level Let's Climb Bible Study Ministry. Bathroom cleaning was his first ministry assignment.

He is a graduate of the Jamaica Theological Seminary and holds a Bachelor's Degree in Theology, with a minor in Guidance and Counselling. He acquired a diploma in Biblical Principles from Victory Bible School, and a certificate from the International Accelerated Missions School (IAMS). Rev. Morrison is married and has four sons and one daughter.

**NOTE:** For feedback, consultation or speaking engagements contact Rev. Morrison at restorativeauthor@gmail.com. Kindly submit a review on Amazon or the platform where you bought this book. Thank you.

# MARITAL INTIMACY

Made in the USA
Columbia, SC
26 July 2022